W9-AOH-886

FROGGY LEARNS TO SWIM

FROGGY LEARNS TO SWIM

by JONATHAN LONDON
illustrated by FRANK REMKIEWICZ

PUFFIN BOOKS

For pollywogs Aaron, Sean, and Yasha —
who learned to swim together;
and for Froggy's mother, Maureen
— J. L.

For Madeleine
— F. R.

PUFFIN BOOKS
Published by the Penguin Group
Penguin Putnam Books for Young Readers,
 345 Hudson Street, New York, New York 10014, U.S.A.
Penguin Books Ltd, 27 Wrights Lane, London W8 5TZ, England
Penguin Books Australia Ltd, Ringwood, Victoria, Australia
Penguin Books Canada Ltd,
 10 Alcorn Avenue, Toronto, Ontario, Canada M4V 3B2
Penguin Books (N.Z.) Ltd,
 182-190 Wairau Road, Auckland 10, New Zealand

Penguin Books Ltd, Registered Offices:
Harmondsworth, Middlesex, England

First published in the United States of America by
 Viking, a division of Penguin Books USA Inc., 1995
Published in Puffin Books, 1997

40 39 38

Text copyright © Jonathan London, 1995
Illustrations copyright © Frank Remkiewicz, 1995
All rights reserved

THE LIBRARY OF CONGRESS HAS CATALOGED THE VIKING EDITION AS FOLLOWS:
London, Jonathan.
Froggy learns to swim / by Jonathan London;
illustrated by Frank Remkiewicz. p. cm.
Summary: Froggy is afraid of the water until his mother, along
with his flippers, snorkle, and mask, help him learn to swim.
ISBN 0-670-85551-0
[1. Swimming—Fiction. 2. Fear—Fiction.
3. Frogs—Fiction. 4. Mothers and sons—Fiction.]
I. Remkiewicz, Frank, ill. II. Title.
PZ7.L8432Frl 1995 [E]—dc20 94–43077 CIP AC

Puffin Books ISBN 978-0-14-055312-3

Manufactured in China

It was hot.
"It's a great day for a swim!"
said Froggy's mother.
So Froggy and his parents
flopped outside to the pond—*flop flop flop*.

"On your mark . . . get set . . . *go!*"
Froggy's father sailed in—*splash!*
Froggy's mother sailed in—*splash!*
But where was Froggy?

FRRROOGGYY! called his mother.

"Wha-a-a-at?"

"Come on in and swim!"

"No! No! I don't know how to swim!
I want to *swing!*"

"*Whee!*"
sang Froggy,
swinging
higher and higher.
He swung so high
he almost touched the sky.

He swung so high
he wound round and round
the crossbar—*zzziiinnnggg*—

then unwound like a spring—
zzzziiiiinnnnnggggggg—

and flew through the air . . .

right smack into the pond—*splash!*

"What are you do-o-o-ing?"
asked Froggy's mother.

"I'm drow-w-w-ning," cried Froggy. *"He-l-l-l-p!"*

He grabbed hold of his mother and climbed on.

"What do you mean you're drowning?
Don't you know frogs are born in the water?
They are *great* swimmers!"

"Not me!" bubbled Froggy.
"I can't swim!"

"Oh fiddlesticks!" she said.
"I'll show you how."

"First, float on your belly
and stick your face in—
I won't let go.

Say, 'Bubble bubble,'
under water.
Then raise your
face for air
and say, 'Toot toot.'"

"I don't want to," Froggy whined.

"Oh come on, Froggy, just try it.
Repeat after me: 'Bubble bubble, toot toot.'"

"Bubble bubble, toot toot!" spluttered Froggy.

"Great! Now float on your back and do the frog kick—I won't let go. Then go like this."

And she showed
Froggy how, saying:
"Chicken . . .
airplane . . .
soldier.

Do it, and repeat after me:
'Chicken . . .
airplane . . .
soldier.'"

"I don't want to," whined Froggy.

"Oh come on, Froggy, just try it!"

"Chicken . . . airplane . . . soldier," gasped Froggy.
He glubbed and blubbed and almost sank.
"Mommy! I need my flippers.
Then I'll swim."

Froggy climbed out
and flopped back to his house.

He pulled on his flippers—*zup!*—

and flopped back to the pond—*flop flop . . . splash!*

"Now try it again," said Froggy's mother.

"Bubble bubble, toot toot.
Chicken, airplane, soldier."
He glubbed and blubbed and almost sank.
"Mommy! I need my mask and snorkel.
Then I'll swim!"

Froggy climbed out
and flopped back to his house.

He pulled on his mask and snorkel—*zook! zik!*—

and flopped back to the pond—*flop flop . . . splash!*

"Now one more time,"
said Froggy's mother.

"Bubble bubble, toot toot.
Chicken, airplane, soldier."

And then it happened.
"Oops!" spluttered Froggy.

"What's the matter?" asked his mother.

"Oh, *nothing*," he said, looking more red in the face than green.

"Well, it's getting cold, Froggy.
It's time to get out."

"No, no! I *can't* get out!"

"Why not?"

Then he burst up for air and yelled, "Wait!"

"What *is* it?" asked his mother.

MY BATHING SUIT!

he shouted.
"Don't look!
I'm getting out!"

Froggy climbed out
and yanked on his bathing suit
with a *zap!* of elastic.

Then he pulled on his flippers—*zup!*—

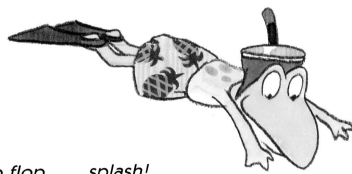

and sailed back into the pond—*flop flop . . . splash!*

FRRROOGGYY!

called his mother.

Froggy's mother shook her head.
"I *told* you frogs are great swimmers!" she said,
and sat down with Froggy's father to watch him.

. . . all night long.
Zzzwimmmmmmmmm . . .